THE WOLF

The Wolf

Steven **Herrick**

Front Street
Asheville, North Carolina

Also by Steven Herrick

By the River

Originally published in Australia
by Allen & Unwin, 2006
Copyright © 2006 by Steven Herrick
All rights reserved
Printed in China
Designed by Helen Robinson
First U.S. edition

Library of Congress Cataloging-in-Publication Data
Herrick, Steven.
The wolf / Steven Herrick.
p. cm.
Summary: Sixteen-year-old Lucy, living in the shadow of
her violent father, experiences a night of tenderness, danger,
and revelation as she and Jake, her fifteen-year-old neighbor,
search for a legendary wolf in the Australian outback.
ISBN-13: 978-1-932425-75-8 (hardcover : alk. paper)
[1. Fathers and daughters—Fiction. 2. Family problems—
Fiction. 3. Australia—Fiction.] I. Title.
PZ7.H43214Wo 2007
[Fic]—dc22   2006012072

Front Street
An Imprint of Boyds Mills Press, Inc.
A Highlights Company

815 Church Street
Honesdale, Pennsylvania 18431

When I was eighteen, I told Mum I wanted to be a writer. The next day, she went out and bought me a desk and a chair from a secondhand furniture store.

Nearly thirty years on, I still write my books at that desk.

Mum died last year.

I like writing at her desk. It brings us closer.

With love.

—S.H.

1 LUCY

Lucy

My name's Lucy Harding.
Lucy's not short for anything,
it's just Lucy.
That's right, with a "y."
Only people from the city
spell it with an "i,"
or call themselves Lucienne.
I'm not French,
and I'm not from the city.
I'm from Battle Farm.
My grandma named it that,
on account of her always saying,
"It's a battle to keep this place;
a battle to survive."
And she did pretty good.
At surviving, I mean.
She died a few years ago,
aged ninety-two.
She's buried up the hill
next to Grandpa,
overlooking their farm
and I reckon she's up there
thinking,
"Why did my daughter marry
someone like him?
Mr. Right.
He's never right. He just thinks he is."
He is Dad,
but I don't want to talk about him.

Swampland

There are two farms in this valley.
No one else can be bothered
cutting through the ragged paperbarks,
the Paterson's curse,
and the creeping lantana.
Wolli Creek flows deep into the valley
through a sandy swamp,
alive with mosquitoes and bugs.
From the banks, big granite boulders
step up to the hills.
Nothing for farming.
Everyone at school says
we live in the ass-end of the earth.
They all tell stories about
diseased feral animals prowling,
quicksand that swallows you whole,
and strange lights hovering above the bog.
Sometimes, when I'm bored, I join in.
I tell the little kids
about long-winged bats
and wild pigs, big as lions,
and blood-curdling screams at midnight.
It's all I can do to stop from laughing,
but, hell,
it passes the time.

The Hardings

So there's me.
I'm sixteen.
And my mum,
who milks our cow, Martha,
and cooks what she grows,
scraping dirt off potatoes and carrots,
washing them in the sink.
Every evening after dinner
she sits on the back veranda
looking up at her parents' graves.
She doesn't say much
and that suits me fine.
And there's Peter, my brother,
who's twelve, but acts like he's eight.
You know, always pestering me,
or playing shoot-'em-up games on his PlayStation.
Once, he climbed up on the shed roof
in his Superman cape.
Yeah, no kidding.
I bet you're thinking
he jumped off and broke his arm.
Right?
Wrong.
Superman was scared.
Mum got the ladder
and she sent me up
to help him down.
I had to talk all nice and careful,

like I was worried.
"Come on, Peter. It'll be all right.
Superman can't die."
Dad kept fiddling with his car.
That's all he ever does.
Tinker with the engine,
shoot his rifle at targets,
and go on about
everything I do wrong.

The death of poor Winnie

If Peter thinks he's Superman,
Dad acts like some
straight-shooting outlaw.
He sets himself
on the old vinyl car seat against the gum tree
and he gets Peter to draw pictures,
rabbits and deer and kangaroos,
on big sheets of paper.
Then he sticks them on the shed
and fires away.
Does he hit the target?
Well, he hits the shed, at least.
Except one time,
when he had way too much to drink.
I sat under the house
hoping he'd shoot his foot off.
Now *that* would be funny.
He blasted away,
doing his best to hit the mark
but he missed everything
except Winnie, the pig.
You should have heard Superman cry.
Mum rang Mr. Samuels, the town butcher,
who drove out and cut up poor Winnie.
We had pork for dinner
and bacon for breakfast,
every day for a month.
It's the only time
I can remember the old bastard
doing anything useful.

Questions

When Dad's head is so far under the hood,
I imagine walking up behind,
giving him one swift kick
and running away,
never coming back.
But not Peter.
He tries to help.
He hangs around,
shuffling his feet in the dirt,
picking up tools,
leaning over the engine,
asking questions.
Dad only ever answers
with a grunt or a shrug.
Peter keeps talking,
jabber jabber jabber.
Dad lifts his head and frowns,
spits in the dirt,
and picks up another wrench
as he's forced to listen to his own son.
If that was me doing all the talking,
he'd tell me,
straightaway,
to piss off.

I lounge around,
pretending I'm reading,
listening to Peter

and knowing that my stupid father
doesn't know how to shut him up.
"Keep talking, Peter,"
I whisper to myself.
"Ask another question.
Go on."

Lucy, and the work

Mostly I stay out of his way.
Simple as that.
At dinner I eat quicker than I should
and keep my head down.
Whenever anybody asks me
to get the cordial from the fridge
or the salt from the pantry,
I do it without a word.
Don't think I'm weak.
I'm not.
I'm snarling underneath
and they know it.
I'm doing what I'm told to avoid getting hit.

When Grandma was alive
Dad would take his dinner outside
because she stared him down.
Grandma said what she liked.
She wasn't afraid of anything.
She'd grin across the table.

"You don't own nothing, Lucy,
unless you work for it.
Remember that.
Working is the owning."
She'd look at Mum,
daring her to say something,
but no one crossed Grandma.

Some people die

In the last year of her life
Grandma could barely walk.
Every morning she'd struggle out to the veranda,
one arm around my shoulder,
her shaky hand holding a walking stick.
There she'd sit, watching the farm.
He'd keep out of the way,
in the shed or out the back,
smoking one fag after another.
Grandma knew what went on.
She waved her stick at him
whenever he came near.
She'd tell my mum to stand up to him,
to fight back.
Mum was deaf to all that.
When Grandma couldn't leave her bed,
a week before she died,
I sat beside her.
She asked me to draw back the curtains
and open the window,
so she could see up the hill
to Grandpa's grave.
I stayed with her for hours
on the faded old lounge chair,
ready to help if she needed water
or her pills.
It was safe there.
One morning, Grandma heard Dad shouting.

She reached for my hand,
squeezing tight each time his voice
stormed through the walls.
She said, "Lucy, some people die
long before they're in the ground."

Lucy's will

I don't believe in omens
or signs and stuff like that.
But every morning,
before I get out of bed,
I lean over to look at Beaumont Hill,
rising above our farm
like a wild animal about to pounce.
If there's a dark cloud behind the hill
I stay in bed for five more minutes,
waiting to see if the wind blows it past.
I close my eyes
and picture the cloud
moving away from our farm
with the westerly.
If I open my eyes too soon
I know that cloud will stay there all day.
It doesn't mean bad luck.
He'll be in a crappy mood,
cloud or no cloud.
Nothing can change that.
I close my eyes and focus
on the darkness drifting away.
By force of will
I want to move the cloud.
That would be some trick,
if I could do it.

The witness

Ranting, yelling, stomping
around their bedroom.
Sometimes she answers back
and I hear his voice change:
deeper, menacing.

It's the quiet that scares me.

I pull the blankets tight
and hide in my dark cocoon
waiting for another explosion.
I should help Mum, somehow,
be on her side.
But she does nothing to stop it.
"Just keep out of his way, Lucy."
As if it's our fault;
as if we made him like this.

She takes it without a whimper,
too scared to move.
And when he starts on me
in the daylight,
she just looks away
and I'm thinking,
She's just glad it's not her.

I'm not sure what hurts more,
his ugly words,
his backhanders,
or watching Mum seeing it all
and doing nothing.

Floating

I got the idea
when I helped Superman
get down off the roof.
When I want to escape,
I climb the wooden ladder
onto the shed roof
and lie back on the iron,
looking at the high clouds floating by.
I can hear the farm below me:
the dogs growling,
the click of each peg
as Mum hangs the washing,
Dad coughing, sniffing,
lighting another smoke;
Peter talking to anyone who'll listen,
or when that doesn't work,
talking to himself.
I know they can't see me,
they don't even miss me.
I close my eyes
and imagine the clouds, feather-soft,
holding me high above everything.
My body tingles.
I'm alone, if only for a while.
I stay here until the sun fades
behind Beaumont Hill,
when Mum calls me to help with dinner.
I stand and stretch my arms

open to the valley.
On a good day I can almost fool myself
that I belong here.

Preparing dinner

Mum washes the potatoes in the sink,
scrubbing the dirt loose with a plastic brush.
I peel them, ready for the boiling water,
and stare out the window at him
sitting on the seat,
his head tilting forward as he dozes.
"Just stay out of his way."
Mum's so caught up in her work
she doesn't know she's said it aloud.
"What?"
"Nothing, I was just …"
"You were talking about him, weren't you?"
She turns away from the sink,
drying her hands on her apron,
getting the cutlery from the drawer.
"What if he comes after me, Mum?
How do I get out of his way then?"
"Lucy …"
"It's a bit hard to escape
when he's blocking the doorway, don't you reckon?"
She sets the table with nervous hands,
taking extra care with each knife and fork;
anything to avoid answering me.
She shakes her head.
"I don't want to fight, Lucy."
Bloody hell.
I chuck the peeler in the sink
and storm past her.
"Neither do I, Mum."

JAKE 2

Jake

I'm Jake.
Jake Jackson.
I'm fifteen years old.
I live in an old timber house
a stone's throw from Wolli Creek.
Mum and Dad and me have lived here forever.
My Great-grandpa Ellis wandered into this area
with a few prize Merinos and two dogs
and the story goes
that he met Miss Lizzy Beacher
in town one day
when he was asking directions to the barber.
"I wanted a neat trim haircut
and I ended up with a wife.
Best advice I ever got!"
They had lots of kids
and all of them worked on this farm
just like we do now,
and we always will.

The farmhouse

When I was ten years old,
Dad and me built the veranda
around this old place that's stood here
for a hundred years
and we used hardwood from the forest
just like Great-grandpa did.
Dad and me worked for weeks
coating the floorboards in oil,
breathing in the strong smell
mixing with the timber.
Before I stained the last board,
in the far corner by the drainpipe,
Dad got a long sharp nail
and said,
"Scrape our names,
yours and mine,
deep in the grain, with the date.
Your kids, Jake,
my grandkids,
will know what we've built was for them."

Daybreak

Every morning I'm up at daybreak.
I go out to the veranda,
pull my boots on,
and walk down to the hen house.
The frost-hard grass crackles under my feet.
I unlock the gate to the shed
and walk across the dusty floor,
messy with straw and wild grass stalks,
to collect the eggs, still warm,
from the raised nests along the wall.
The hens scatter,
clucking and fussing in the dirt.
Once I saw a two-meter red-belly black snake
curled in the corner of the shed,
near the water trough.
I backed out quickly and ran to tell Dad.
He reached for the shovel
we always keep on the veranda.

We buried the snake behind the shed.
I made a little white cross with a bad rhyme:
Here lies a snake, black and red,
came looking for eggs, now he's dead.

Bread

Sometimes, late in the afternoon,
Mum and I cook in the kitchen.
When I was young she taught me
how to knead the dough for bread.
I love rolling the firm ball in my hands,
sprinkling the flour,
adding the rainwater,
kneading on the big wooden table.
I stack the small-cut logs in the firebox
to make it good and hot,
ready for the loaves.
We got an electric stove years ago
but Mum never cooks bread in that.
"No smoke, no flavor," she says.
Three times a week
we fire up the Early Kooka
to make bread.
And just before dinner
she tears bits off a still-warm loaf,
steaming in her hands.
I get the crust,
smothered in butter
melting in the soft flesh.

The wolf story

Ever since I can remember,
my dad has talked about the wolf.
From the age of five,
I'd sit beside him on the back step.
We'd look across the paddocks of sheep
into the forest shimmering in the afternoon heat,
watching,
the two of us sure the wolf would come
if we sat here long enough.
As night fell,
I'd ask him to tell me,
once more,
about when he saw the wolf.
If the wolf wouldn't show
at least we could talk about him.
In the gathering dark
I'd hang on every word,
listening to Dad's deep voice
tell me
the wolf story.

The wolf at Wolli Creek

"I was twenty years old
when I saw the wolf at Wolli Creek.
I was fishing for trout at Mercer Bend
where the water runs deep and brown,
with bubbles rising to the surface.
I heard a branch snap upstream.

"His head was large and noble.
His ears, bigger than any dog's,
pricked, waiting for a sound.
I stood stock-still as he came down to the creek,
not taking his eyes from me.
As he approached, the forest hushed.
The tips of his fur were lighter in color
and it gave him a ghostly appearance.
His paws sank deep into the wet sand as he drank,
his long tongue lapping the water."

"What next, Dad? What happened?"

"We stared at each other, eye to eye.
It seemed so long, Jake,
but it was probably only a few seconds.
Then he turned and ran into the bushes.
I never saw him again.
But I think of him out there,
maybe with a mate, and a litter.
Wolves don't live in Australia,
so they say."

Jake's shed

Dad and I built the hen house
when I was twelve.
We worked for two days
sawing the heavy posts,
coating them with sump oil.
Dad taught me how to set them level.
I loved hammering the wirc,
bending the nails to hold each end tight,
bashing away without a care.
It didn't seem like work at all.
Even though it was made of scrap iron
and chicken wire,
we knew it'd stand forever
because of the effort we put in;
the care we took to get everything right.
Mum painted the hen house door
a rich green,
as a background,
and with her fine art brushes
she drew our old farmhouse
with smoke rising from the chimney,
hens and chickens pecking in the grass.
"To make them feel at home," she said.
And if you look really closely,
in the corner of the painting,
peeking from behind the house,
you can see a wolf:
a gray wolf.

When Mum finished,
she winked at me.
"For your father, Jake."

HOLIDAYS

3

Jake: the school bus

I walk up the bumpy winding driveway,
jump our wooden double gate,
and wait for the bus.
It's late, as usual.
The clouds roll in over the hills,
cockatoos screech in the dead trees
and the wind blows cold through my jacket.
I chuck a few rocks
at the Eggs for Sale sign
I made ages ago.
We've had two buyers in three years.
Nobody drives down this road except us,
the Hardings,
and the school bus.
It rattles down the road
and squeaks to a stop
with the front door already open.
I hop on,
say hello to Peter and Lucy in the front seat,
and sit behind them.
Every morning it's the same—
before the bus moves,
Peter turns and starts talking.

"Today is the last day of school.
Next week I'm gonna ride me bike every day
and maybe Dad'll loan me his gun
and I'll go shooting.

You wanna come?
We can get a wild pig,
or maybe a fox.
Whaddya reckon, Jake?"

On and on until the bus pulls into school.

Lucy: the Trobriands

I read a book a week.
I don't care what sort of book.
As long as old Mrs. Bains lets me loan it,
I'll read it.
Today I finished a book
about these islands in the South Pacific,
with palm trees and coconuts
and sandy beaches and canoes
and all the heavenly things you'd expect.
But on this island they have a celebration:
a Yam Festival.
It goes for two months,
and all the islanders have sex with each other,
whether they're married or not.
And the young women form gangs
and they rape the men.
No kidding.
Five of them hold him down,
and one jumps on top.
The writer didn't say what the men think of this,
other than they're all a bit scared
to walk alone during the festival.
Now I'm reading this in the library
and I start laughing out loud
about these big strong island men
afraid to walk along a beach or through the forest
because a bunch of young girls like me
might jump out and rape them.

At the end of the festival,
they all go back to being married couples
and the young women
return to working in the village,
waiting for a husband.

Everyone gets married in the Trobriands.

And everyone goes crazy for two months a year.

Jake: in class

Coomuya Central School has seven teachers
for classes Prep to Year Twelve.
Which means sometimes Peter, Lucy, and me
are in the same class
even though we're at different levels.
Mrs. Clarke roams around each desk,
hands behind her back,
grinding her teeth as we work.
The rule is you put your hand up
if you don't understand anything.
Simple.

As soon as we start math,
Peter raises his hand.
Mrs. Clarke explains it once again,
leaning down to write the formula
in his workbook.
She circles the classroom,
the click of her heels loud on the timber floor,
until Peter calls,
"But, Miss …?"
his hand held high.
This goes on all morning.
It's perfect.
Those of us who want to work, do it.
Those who want to doodle on their books
can draw for as long as they want.
Peter is the most popular kid in class,
for all the wrong reasons.

Lucy: the library

Stupid old Mrs. Bains only lets us
take out three books over the holidays.
It's nowhere near enough.
So, every day this week
I've picked a book I want
and taken it to the back corner of the library,
well away from Bains and her hawk eyes.
I settle on the beanbag,
acting like I'm absorbed in the book,
but really I'm waiting for her phone to ring.
Bains has this weird habit
of closing her eyes when she talks on the phone.
I reckon she's deaf
and her fuzzy old brain thinks
that if her eyes are shut
then her ears will be open.
I don't know and I don't care.
But when she's talking, she can't see me.
I sneak open the back window,
place the book on the ledge
and head out of the library.
I race around the back and pick up the book.
My long-term loan.

Jake: last day of term

The last day of school
before the winter holidays.
Mrs. Clarke is chirpier than usual.
She gets the class to read aloud
from this book about an old bloke
who thinks he's in a prisoner of war camp.
We all laugh when he hides under the bed
"cursing the Japs"
as the nurses spend hours searching the grounds.
Everyone in class wants Mrs. Clarke to read,
but she insists we do.
The book goes round from desk to desk,
one page each ...
Peter reads so slowly.
Everyone stares out the window
at the cleaner emptying bins,
at the Primary kids playing cricket,
at the cows in a distant paddock,
as we try to follow the story ...
one painful, mispronounced word at a time.

Mrs. Clarke thanks Peter for his effort
and asks me to take over.
I'm eager to see if the old fellow escapes the home.
I cross the fingers of my left hand
as thanks to Mum for teaching me to read,
so I won't be shamed
like Peter Harding
staring straight at the chalkboard.

Lucy: disgust

I hate it when Clarkie does that.
I reckon it's payback
for all the questions he asks in math.

Peter can't read for nothing.
She shouldn't make him.
Everyone in class lounging around,
groaning
or looking out the window,
listening to him stammer over simple words,
all because he got genes from Dad,
who wouldn't know what a book is for.
I've seen him rip out pages
to use as fire-starters
for our old woodstove in the kitchen.
At home I hide my books
under the wardrobe in my room
and read them late at night,
while the dogs bark
and Dad opens another bottle.
Dad says,
"You don't need books, girl.
To be smart, all you need is what's up here."
And he taps his head
with a nicotine finger.
He means a brain, but
I so want to say,
"What? Dirty hair?"

Lucy: three weeks

I'm thinking of nothing but holidays
as I walk out the school gate
to wait for the bus.
Three weeks away from this place,
reading books by Wolli Creek
and dreaming of places I'd like to go.
The creek is far enough away
so I don't hear Dad shouting at Mum,
or hear Peter whining, bored,
or the dogs growling over leftover bones,
and the constant bark of talkback radio
and know-all announcers raving on
about the economy
and refugees,
the unemployed,
the Aborigines,
and on and on
and Dad hanging around outside,
smoking rollies,
saying, "He's right, you know!"
to every stupid thing he hears.
I'd like to pitch a tent beside Wolli Creek
and live there,
listening to the gentle sound
of clear water bubbling over rocks.

Lucy: on holidays

On the bus home,
Nathan Stokes,
a seat behind us,
mocks Peter's reading,
mimics his words,
stuttering,
looking for an audience.
Peter's hands are shaking
and I'm not sure if he's going to cry
or start screaming,
and either way
I don't want to be part of this crap.
So, I turn and face Stokes.
I don't say anything.
I just give him a killer look
until even Nathan Stokes
is not sure if it's worth the effort of going on.
I see him searching for help.
He's about to try his luck,
so I lean in close
and slap him hard across the face.
The slap echoes down the bus
and no one moves until our stop.
I pick up my bag,
saunter down the aisle
and step off onto the road.
When the bus turns,
Nathan calls after Peter,

"You wait, Harding.
You can't always hide behind your sister."
Big, strong Peter
gives Nathan the finger
as I stroll up our long dirt driveway,
on holidays.

Jake: on holidays

I skirt the western boundary
with Patch bounding ahead
chasing the swallows
and barking at the clouds.
Spud ambles beside me,
tongue out, tail wagging.
I check the fence,
feel the tension in the wire,
the strength of the posts,
firm in the ground.
I remember working the post-hole digger,
hoping there were no rocks underneath
as we dug into the brown soil.
It took two weeks last winter
with the winds ripping down the valley.
Sometimes I imagine
I can still feel the cracks in my hands,
deep and hard.
Patch drops a stick at my feet
and jumps away,
eyes flashing between me
and the lure of the prize.
I fling the stick
and sit against the post.
Spud nuzzles his head into my chest,
wanting to be scratched behind his ears.
I rub my hands deep into his fur.
Patch drops his new toy at my feet, again.
The three of us in the sunshine,
on holidays.

Lucy: dinner

It's the last time
I do anything for my stupid brother.
He didn't have to tell everyone what I did,
and bullshit about
how he was going to hit Stokes himself,
if I hadn't done it first.
Sure, Superman, sure.
And all the time he's talking
I know Dad's watching me,
waiting for the chance …
"So, your sister *can* fight back, Peter?"
I shovel in the food,
quick as it'll go.
I just want out of here.
And Peter says,
"I would have punched him, Dad.
Not just a slap."
I bite down hard on my food
to keep from reaching across the table
to shut him up myself.
"Only girls slap, Dad."

I can't take it anymore.
"Yeah, and only boys are cowards with fists."
As soon as the words are out,
I know I've said too much.
I carry my plate to the sink, to rinse,
sure his eyes haven't left me.

I hear him get up
and slowly walk around the table
to stand behind me.
He says,
"These hands work this farm, girl."
He's waiting.
If I turn to face him he'll hit me,
so I wash my plate,
keeping my head down,
my shoulders stiff,
hands shaking under the flow of the water.
He says,
"She's not so tough now, Peter."

Peter

My dad, he gets angry sometimes.
I don't know what for.
Maybe it's because of the farm
and not having no money and stuff.
Or maybe it's 'cause he wishes
he was a truckie,
which was his job before he met Mum.
He was just driving through town,
delivering stuff.
When he told me that
he snapped his fingers and said,
"Like that, from truckie to farmer."
And he clicked his fingers again
to prove how quick things change.
Then he goes quiet for a real long time
as if he's back driving across the country,
with no one around and nothing to worry about.
I try and cheer him up by telling him
I've made the cricket team at school,
and asking about the farm
and whether we should plant some crops
and hope for better luck this year.
I reckon I'll be a farmer one day.
Only I'll try and not get too angry,
even if we don't make money
or have much to do way out here.

Jake: chasing ghosts

This morning I boil the eggs,
and wait for Mum and Dad
to come in from the bottom paddock.
Dad chucks his hat on the table
and wipes his sleeve across his forehead.
He swears under his breath.
Another sheep is dead.

I put the toast on his plate
and an egg in the cup, ready.
Mum sets the old kettle on the stove.
"Second sheep this week, Jake.
If this keeps up,
there'll be no shearing this season.
None."

"It's a fox, Dad."
"No way, Jake.
The sheep was ripped to bits.
Foxes eat their fill and leave.
This animal's bigger.
I followed his paw prints down to the creek.
He's a smart animal, this wolf."

I don't answer.
I know Dad and his endless search for the wolf.
"Are we spotlighting tonight, Dad?"
He sighs.
"I spend my days burying sheep
and my nights chasing ghosts."

Jake: spotlighting

Patch and Spud jump on the pickup
as Dad loads his gun,
flicks on the safety switch,
and carefully places it along the rack
behind the seat.
I climb on the back
and grip the spotlight on the roof.
My knees press into the old mattress
wedged against the cabin
so the bumping and shaking
over the paddocks won't toss me.
Dad starts the engine
and the dogs start barking.
It's a clear, crisp night with hundreds of stars
and I can smell the smoke
from the Hardings' fireplace.
Dad drives slowly and keeps to the tracks,
his hands tugging the wheel
to miss the potholes.
The pickup bounces along
as I direct the spotlight,
this way and that.
Its murderous stare
stabs deep into the scrub.
We both see something
reflecting from the bush,
glinting in the beam.
Dad reaches for the rifle,

eyes never leaving the light,
until he sees it's a kangaroo
dazzled by the brightness.
Dad could take him out with one shot.
Patch and Spud bark,
but their leads hold firm.
The 'roo bounds through the bush
and Dad drives on.

Jake: midnight

After an hour of searching
and rattling over sheep tracks,
Dad parks by the creek
and kills the engine.
I let Patch and Spud off their leads.
They jump from the pickup
and dash for the creek,
tails flipping like wild antennae.
Dad and I sit on the warm hood
as we unwrap the sandwiches.
He pours tea into the tin mugs
and we look up at the stars.

"I used to count them
when I was your age, Jake.
I could never keep tally.
There's just too many."
"Like possums, rabbits, and 'roos," I reply.
"Lucky they live here.
Harding would use them for target practice."
Dad has no time for the Hardings
and their farm with overgrown weeds
and stock that run wild,
knocking down fences
and fouling the creek.

Dad never kills anything,
except foxes and snakes.

Foxes kill sheep.
Snakes kill people.
So Dad kills foxes and snakes.
Simple as that.

But here we are spotlighting,
gun loaded,
hunting.
"If it's really the wolf, Dad,
what are you going to do if we see it?"
"What do you want me to do, Jake?
Let it kill my sheep?"
"I couldn't pull the trigger," I say,
"not if it's really a wolf. I mean,
they don't live …"
Dad interrupts. "Yeah, I know.
They don't live in Australia.
So, maybe all the more reason to shoot it."
"You'd kill it?
To prove it's here? That's crazy."
Dad slides off the hood
and packs the cooler,
screwing the lid on the thermos so tight
I can hear the thread scraping.
"I don't know, Jake.
Let's find the bloody thing first."
"What do we do then?"
Dad ignores my question,

chucks the cooler in the back,
whistles for the dogs,
and starts the engine.
He winds down the window.
"You coming?
Or staying out here with the wolf?"

Lucy: Christmas

It was Christmas Day
last year
and we were in the backyard
after lunch.
For the first time
in a long while
he hadn't raised his voice all day
or complained about the food
or said anything nasty to me.
He was sitting under the tree
polishing his gun
and taking potshots
at the shed
and Peter's drawings.
A kookaburra landed on a branch
a few meters above him
and let out a thrilling laugh
that seemed to echo off the hills
and fill the valley.
I was so happy watching the bird
and marveling at its noise,
I didn't see Dad raise the gun
and fire.
All I saw
was the bird fall at his feet.
He looked at me and said,
"He's not laughing now."
I've never heard the valley so quiet.

The moment after he killed the bird.
Dead quiet.

When he went inside,
I walked across to the kookaburra,
picked it up, and
took its body behind the shed.
I dug a deep grave
and buried him
where the dogs can't get him.

4 LONESOME HOWL

Jake: the lonesome howl

It's a lonesome howl,
echoing across the valley.
I jump out of bed,
eager,
opening the window wide
so I can lean out into the chill night.
Darkness.
The gum tree scratches against the window.
The faint light of the moon
reflects off the iron of the hen house
and another howl floats across the valley,
long and lonely.
It's so mournful I can feel it on my skin.
He's searching for a mate,
marking his territory.
I close my eyes.
He's high on Beaumont Hill,
his head cocked arrow-straight at the moon
as he lets loose this deep wail
over the forest
and the winter paddocks.
Both of us, the wolf and me,
under a half moon,
waiting for a reply that never comes.

Lucy: wild dog

Years ago, Grandma told me
the story of the dog turned wild.
I was at school when it happened.
One of our dogs, Shadow,
was sleeping under the stairs
when Dad walked down
and trod on his tail.
Shadow woke in fright
and bit Dad on the leg
and wouldn't let go.
Grandma was smiling
as she told me about Dad shouting,
lashing out at the dog,
but Shadow locked onto his leg,
growling,
as if possessed by ancient blood.
Grandma said Dad beat that dog
over and over across his back
until he let go,
growling still,
circling him in the dirt.
Shadow was boss of the yard
until Dad fled inside and got the gun.
He raced back outside,
swearing, calling the dog's name
and trying to load the gun,
all at the same time.
Shadow was too quick.

He ran across the paddocks.
Dad chased him for hours
and never got close.
Grandma told me she loved that dog
and she was sure Dad heard Shadow's howls
and remembered being defeated
in his own backyard.

Lucy: my friend

I hear the howl
and close my book.
My friend, the wild dog.
He's up on Beaumont Hill, I reckon,
looking for a mate,
or just howling because he can.
He's not scared of anything
because he's the boss
and every other animal hears that call
and keeps out of his way.
Like at school,
when Jim Bradley swaggers across the oval.
Everyone moves aside
because he's bigger and meaner
and he likes to fight.
We all just back off
and let Jim go where he wants.
It's no skin off my nose.
He can bully all he likes,
so long as he leaves me alone.
Only Jim Bradley is not like the wild dog.
He's not nearly as smart.
There's the call again.
I go to my window
and see the heavy clouds over Beaumont Hill.
I'd like to be up there now,
looking down on everything
in the forest night,
where no one can touch you.

Jake: breakfast

"I'd rather he howled all night
than ripped apart my sheep."
That's what Dad says in the morning
while we eat breakfast on the veranda,
looking up at the dark clouds
covering the rocky hills
all around our valley.
"I haven't heard him for ages, Dad."
"Me neither. But now we know he's still around.
I'd hoped he'd move north for winter."
"What, like a surfie wolf?"
Mum chuckles into her toast.
"Very funny, Jake.
I don't care what he does,
as long as I have the same number of sheep
each morning."

Dad tosses the tea leaves into the garden
and goes inside.
I shiver, pull my jacket tight
and watch the chickens pecking at the scraps.
One day, I'll find the wolf.
Face to face,
we'll see each other across Wolli Creek
and he'll know I've been waiting,
searching for him all my life.

I'll hold out my hand,
tell him I understand his howl
echoing through the night.

Then he'll be my wolf.

Lucy: breakfast

Dad walks into the kitchen,
carrying his .22 and a box of bullets.
He drags out his chair
and starts loading the magazine,
looking up,
waiting for someone to ask where he's going.
I finish my cereal and stand to leave.
"Your wild dog better watch out, Lucy.
I've had enough of that mangy animal
keeping me awake.
Today he's dead."
I wash my bowl in the sink
and imagine Dad scrambling up Beaumont Hill,
searching and swearing.
He's got as much chance of finding the dog
as he has of finding a job.
As I walk out, I say,
"Yeah. Good luck."
He sits at the table
snapping the magazine into the rifle
and yells after me,
"Nothing to do with luck.
He's dead. You mark my words."
I walk into the backyard
where Mum is hanging the washing.
She looks up as he shouts some more,
then suddenly becomes real interested
in the wet clothes in the basket.

Anything to avoid my eyes.
Mum and me,
sometimes we go for days
not looking at each other.

Peter

Dad's gonna kill the wild dog today.
No worries.
I reckon the dog deserves it,
howling all night
like a ghost.
I'm not scared or nothing.
I just don't like being woke up.
Dad polishes his cool gun
and I wanna go with him.
I got good eyes
and I reckon I could spot the dog
a mile away, easy.
I could point and let Dad have a free shot.
I was gonna ask,
but he was in one of his moods
and Mum said I shouldn't.
She didn't want me chasing Dad all over the hills,
getting in his way when he's got his gun.
She don't know nothing.
I'd help.
I'd find that wild dog.

Lucy: bad luck

I don't remember when it started.
Honest.
One day I was a normal kid,
chasing the hens,
chucking rocks at the crows,
running about the farm
without a care …
The next?
I was bad luck.
I was the cause of the drought,
the bushfire,
the floods.
He was stuck here because of me.
Wasting his life.
Every day he laid into me
with his words,
as though blaming someone else
made it easier for him.
And what he said stung
like a nest of bull ants,
but I'll tell you what hurt more.
Every day while this was going on,
Mum did nothing to stop him.
She kept cooking,
mopping the floor,
hanging the washing.
She seemed to work harder,
to keep quieter,

as I got older.
Maybe she thought the same as him?
That I'd brought them both bad luck,
just by being born.
Maybe she was glad it wasn't Peter
being picked on.
I was the easy target.

I don't remember when it started.
I don't know *why* it started.
But it's never stopped.

I grew my hair long
and let it fall in front of my face,
to hide my eyes from his hate.
To hide my hate from his eyes.

Lucy: crash

I don't want to think about him
hunting the wild dog
so I gather up a bunch of rocks,
golf-ball size.
I take a bucket load
to the far side of the yard.
In the cold sunshine
I chuck them, one at a time,
as high as I can
so they land on the old shed roof
with a loud crash
that makes Mum look up
as she sits on the veranda.
She wants to say something,
but she won't.
I pick up another rock
and throw with all my strength,
watch it arc high over the shed
and land on the house roof
above the veranda.
It rolls down
with a satisfying thump
at the foot of the steps
not far from Mum.
She doesn't say a word
and I say nothing back.

Lucy: beside the creek

Jake and Peter
are on the other side of the creek
so I ignore them.
I read my book,
listening to the magpies
and the distant bleat of sheep.
I haven't heard a gunshot yet.
That makes me smile.
I picture my useless father
struggling through the lantana
all around the hills,
swearing and sweating.
He'll get cut by the bushes
and he'll swear some more.
After hours of this,
he'll sit on a rock and drink his warm beer,
hoping the dog will just walk by.
No chance.
Something on Beaumont Hill
has a brain
and it's not the one drinking beer.
I read my book
and bask in the sun.
I'll stay here all day.
I don't want to be around
when he gets home.
Warm beer, hot sun,
and no dog.

Jake: my dad and your dad

Peter says, "My dad says your dad is a flake.
Wolves don't live in Australia.
It's a wild dog, that's all."
He picks up a flat stone
and skims it across the calm surface of the creek.
"Didn't you hear the howl last night?" I ask.
"Dogs can howl too, you know.
Our dogs howl all night 'cause they're hungry.
My dad says he's going to shoot it,
no questions asked," Peter boasts.
He never shuts up.
"Your dad is weak.
He don't even shoot rabbits.
My dad says if something is on his farm
and it ain't a sheep or a human,
well, it's dead.
Nothing's taking our sheep.
Nothing."

Jake: Lucy Harding

Lucy Harding is still and quiet,
nothing like Peter.
She sits on the bank opposite,
reading, ignoring us.
Her long, black hair
falls in front of her face,
like she's hiding from the world.
She wears jeans every day,
even to school.
And brown riding boots
with worn heels and cuts along the toe.
I wade across Wolli Creek,
stepping from rock to rock,
getting wet up to my knees,
and sit beside Lucy.
She doesn't look up.
I close my eyes,
enjoying the sun,
and the silence away from loudmouth Peter.

"It's not a wolf.
It's just a wild dog."
She hasn't lifted her head from the book.
She spoke so softly
I'm not even sure I've heard right,
so I say,
"The wolf?"
"It's not a wolf, okay."

She lifts her head and looks at me.
Then she says,
"Hell. I don't care.
Call it a wolf, if you want."

Peter

Geez, I hate that Jake Jackson.
Him and me stupid sister
talking about the wolf.
It's like fairy tales and Santa Claus
and dumb Easter bunnies
and stuff that's not even real.
I hate them because they smirk
like they're smarter than me.
And his dad don't even shoot pests.
He lets them live and breed and cause trouble
when this land is for sheep
and nothing else but us farmers.
One day I'm going to find the mangy old hound
that howls at the moon
and drag its dead body
down to the creek here.
Then let's see if Lucy and Jake look so smart,
when they see it ain't nothing but a mangy dog.
Nothing but a dead dog.

Jake: one day

Peter gets bored skimming stones
with no one to babble to,
so he wanders home.
Lucy stays.
I watch the dragonflies
hover above the water.
Crazy helicopters, Dad calls them.
Trout live in the creek, for sure.
And turtles, crayfish,
eels—slippery and dark with oily skin.
Once, when I was fishing,
I dragged ashore an old shoe
full of sand and weed.
It's a good creek though—no carp, or catfish.
The water is filtered clean
in the swamp upstream.
It's deep enough for swimming
and sometimes, in spring, fast enough
to lie on a tractor tube and float for miles
downstream to the Pattaya River.
Sometimes I dream of getting a canoe
and just drifting along,
turning into the great river
and paddling until I reach the coast
hundreds of kilometers away.
Mum once told me that's how the farmers
who lived here during the war
went to the coast to enlist.

It took them two weeks of hard paddling,
but they made it.
They signed on and went overseas to fight.
Some never returned.

Jake: where the wolf lives?

"I know where your wolf lives."
"*What*?"
Lucy doesn't say much,
but she sure knows how to get my attention.
"Where?" I ask.
"Near Balancing Rock
on Sheldon Mountain.
About twelve kilometers from here."

I know the place.
Bare rocks, rounded by time,
and one balancing,
ready to roll off the mountain
and crush whatever is below.
The bush is thick
and it's dark and creepy.
I shiver just thinking about it.
Dad and me went there once
searching for stray sheep.
We wandered around for hours
and found nothing but huge boulders,
stinging nettles, and a rotting carcass.

"How do you know he lives there?" I ask.
Lucy brushes her hair behind her ear
and looks up from her book.
"I just do, that's all," she replies,
her eyes steady on me.

"I'll show you,
if you promise not to tell anyone where we go,
especially Peter."

I think about it for a while.
What if it's true?
I'd want to tell Dad.
Twenty years he's been searching.
"Well?" Lucy asks.
"Okay. I promise."
"Good. We'll go tomorrow.
I'll meet you here, early.
Bring food and water."

I stand to leave.
How can I not tell Dad?
Lucy grabs my arm.
"We keep it quiet. Okay?
Just you and me, Jake."
I look into her eyes.
"Okay, Lucy.
We find the wolf,
but then I tell Dad.
Deal?"
She shrugs and says,
"We find a wolf,
you can tell the bloody world."

THE DEEP SILENCE 5

Lucy: the deep silence

I don't really know
where the wild dog lives.
I've decided I'm getting away from this farm.
So I tell Jake about the rock on Sheldon Mountain.
It's the sort of place a wolf would stand
looking over the whole valley,
looking for a mate,
looking for food.
If I was queen of this valley,
it's where I'd live.
High above everything
where no one ever goes,
where the cloud lingers,
where I can hide away;
where on cold foggy nights
I can sit near the rock
and howl long into the deep silence.

Jake: Dad's wolf

I pick apples
from the wild tree near the track
and take them to our horse, Charlie.
He trots across his yard
and takes an apple from my hand.
I pat his thick mane
as he crunches the fruit.
Lucy and me and the wolf?
All those years of talking about it
and searching for it.
I rub Charlie's smooth back
and listen to Patch and Spud.
Dinnertime.
They always bark
when they smell Mum's cooking,
even if they only get leftovers.
Dad's wolf?
Or mine?
Tomorrow, on Sheldon Mountain,
I'm going to find out.

Jake: roast

"You'll love dinner tonight, Jake.
It's a roast."

"Great, Mum. My favorite!"
Better than Dad's Chicken Surprise,
which is just scrambled eggs.
Dad says, "It could have been a chicken.
That's the surprise."

"It's a special anniversary, Jake," Mum says.
I'm struggling to remember.
"Eighteen years ago today,
your dad and I got married."
Mum laughs at the memory.
"We couldn't afford a honeymoon,
so we cooked a roast.
We moved the table onto the veranda,
opened a bottle of wine,
lit candles,
and had the best dinner."

I go to one end of the kitchen table,
lift, and say,
"Come on, Mum.
It's not too cold for dinner outside."

Jake: dinner on the veranda

"Everyone in town says a wolf
couldn't survive out here
without being shot, or captured," Dad says.
He leans back in the old wooden chair,
rubbing his fingers into his forehead.

"They may be right, Dad."
I'm tempted to tell him about Lucy
and Sheldon Mountain,
but I promised.
"Peter says his dad thinks it's a wild dog.
When he finds it, he's going to shoot it."
Dad frowns and pours another beer.
"He's a rotten shot.
The day I start listening to a Harding …
well, that day will never come."

I don't want to talk about the wolf
since Lucy told me her secret.
"Great dinner, Mum. I'll wash up.
After all, it's your anniversary."
Dad looks at me, laughs, and says,
"I knew there was a reason we had you, Jake."

Lucy: every step I take

When Peter asks Dad
if he shot the wild dog,
I think Dad's going to choke.
All day on Beaumont Hill,
struggling through the bush for nothing.
He shoves back his chair
and burps loudly.
That's his way of saying thanks for dinner.
Mum clears the plates
as Dad storms into the lounge,
calling over his shoulder,
"Lucy, do the dishes."
As if I didn't know.
As if him, or precious Superman,
would ever get their hands wet
doing a household chore.
Mum stands by the sink,
holding a tea towel, waiting.
Dad calls for another beer
above the noise of the television
and she hurries to the fridge.
I'm left alone with the dishes.
That suits me fine.

When I finish
I stand outside looking up at the glowing moon,
rising over the hills.
A newspaper blows across the dirt

and catches on the wire fence.
I'm glad he had such a hard time today.
And tomorrow,
Jake and me are heading
in the opposite direction,
tracking through the swamp
to climb Sheldon Mountain.
Jake will be looking for paw prints,
listening for sounds,
searching the bush,
hoping to catch sight of his wolf
so he can tell his dad.
I'll be walking ahead of him,
whistling
with every step I take
away from this farm.

Lucy: the wish

I want the dog to howl tonight.
To tell everyone who's boss.
I want my dad to hear
and know that it's not afraid of him.
Dad can sit in his chair,
dirty feet on the footstool,
gripping his beer,
staring at the stupid television,
and know that he's a loser.
He can't even find a dog.

Howl, dog.
Howl in his face.
A cold breeze blows down the valley
and the Jacksons' rooster starts crowing.
I once read a book
about these American Indians
who could imitate animal noises.
They would lure their prey in close
by calling it.
What I'd give to do that.
Dad would go crazy.
The wild dog, right outside his window.
Laughing at him.
Laughing in his face.

Jake: late at night

Tonight I Googled "Wolves in Australia."
I got twenty listings for the Wollongong Wolves Soccer
Team
and thirty-six for the movie *Wolf Creek*.
But no wolves in Australia.

No wolves *ever* in Australia.

Someone should tell Dad that,
but it won't be me.
The Web site said wolves don't attack humans
and their average lifespan is twelve years.
Dad's wolf is long dead,
unless, as Dad thinks,
he had a mate and a litter,
which means tomorrow Lucy and I
may be looking for more than one animal.

Or we'll spend all day on Sheldon Mountain
looking for a ghost dog that doesn't exist.

In bed, I listen to the night sounds:
a tree branch rustling against the roof,
the crackling wood in our fireplace,
the dogs on Hardings' farm barking for food.
Our silly rooster starts crowing in the darkness
and then all is quiet.
No howl.
Not a sound.

Lucy: tomorrow

I lie awake most of the night
thinking about me and Jake
searching.
I just want to get as far away from here as I can.
I couldn't care less if we find the dog.
I've got to leave before they wake up,
or else Superman will complain about being bored,
like he does every morning,
and I'll be stuck with him for the day.
Mum will say,
"Go on, Lucy, take him with you.
He won't be any trouble."
I wonder where she's been
for the last twelve years
if she doesn't know that Peter
is nothing but trouble.
All I want to do is keep moving
in a direction away from this farm.
And when it comes time to turn around,
I've got to say to Jake,
"You go back.
But not me.
Not ever."

Lucy: before dawn

It's still dark out.
Dad burps loudly
as he sleeps in the lounge chair.
He rolls over,
knocking the bottle of beer.
It dribbles across the floor,
making a pool at his feet.
I creep to the kitchen
and pack my schoolbag with fruit,
a half loaf of bread, and some cheese.
A pack of stubbies is on the top shelf.
Do I dare steal his only beer?
He'll freak.
My hand is shaking as I take it.
He can drink water, like the rest of us.
I open the back door very quietly
and the dogs start to growl
so I quickly throw them some biscuits.
There's mist over the far paddocks
and the faint rays of first light breaking through.
The dew is shining on the grass
and I can hear the crows in the trees.
Soon Jake will be awake
ready for his big adventure.

Jake: just a bushwalk

This morning I boil two extra eggs
and let them cool while we eat breakfast.
I peel and place them in a bowl,
add a small amount of milk,
lots of cracked pepper,
and mash them all up.
Then I pack the sandwiches into my schoolbag
with water and apples.
"Me and Lucy are going for a bushwalk today."
"Lucy?" Dad looks uncertain.
"Lucy Harding!
You're kidding."

"It's just a bushwalk, Dad."
He says,
"I don't trust them.
I never will."
He pours himself another cup of tea,
slopping the milk on the bench,
and slams the back door
as he goes to the veranda
where Mum waits.
No one can argue with him when he's like this.
He's right, and that's all there is to it.
Or so he thinks.

I shrug into my oilskin jacket.
I don't want to be stuck on Sheldon Mountain

shivering with cold.
I carry the pack outside
and stand on the step.
I want to tell him he's wrong.
That he doesn't know everything.
He doesn't know where the wolf is.
I do.
Dad swills his tea leaves into the garden.
"Don't think you'll be spending all holiday
with a Harding. We've got work to do."
Mum raises her long fingers to her lips,
telling me not to bother arguing.
I walk away.

Jake: a creek apart

Lucy is sitting on the same rock as yesterday.
She's slowly pouring beer into the stream,
one bottle at a time,
and arranging the stack of empties on the bank.

I don't really know her at all ...

I call across Wolli Creek and she waves back.
"I'll meet you at the bridge, upstream," I say.
I don't feel like wading across
and getting soaked,
not with a long hike ahead.
Lucy and I walk along each bank,
glancing across every few seconds.
I feel like a real fool doing this,
separated by the creek.
We reach Hopkins Bridge
and I cross to her side.
She's carrying a schoolbag, like mine.
"Food and water," she says.
"And I stole Dad's beer.
I poured it all into the creek,
while I was waiting for you.
Do you think fish get drunk?"

Jake: the swamp

We follow the creek
for a few kilometers with Lucy leading.
I can see tiny fish darting through the water
as we walk along an old sheep track
overgrown with wild grass.
This leads us into the swamp
and almost immediately
the sun passes behind a cloud.
The path disappears
as we pick our way through the sand and mud
feeling the ooze creep around our boots.
I remember the swamp stories at school.
"Do you believe in the lights, Lucy?"
She scoffs,
leading the way through the marsh.
"Yeah, it's a wild pig with a torch."
Black, biting sand flies buzz around my face
and lodge in my ears.
I slap a bug off my arm.
"This sand is really boggy," I say.
Lucy turns and says,
"It's mud and sand and water,
all mixed up and squelchy.
That's what a swamp is, you know?"
She sure is prickly.
As she turns and strides away,
I imitate her words under my breath
while the sludge seeps into my boots.

Lucy: the swamp

It's the ass-end of the world
and we're walking through it.
I don't believe in the lights
and I've never seen anything
coming out of this swamp but the clean water
that trickles down into Wolli Creek.
I've heard all the stories in town.
I'm not scared.
Let's face it—
if you live in a crap town
and you're going to be stuck there forever,
well, you find a place that's even worse
and you make up stories
and run it down
to build up your own little place.
You'll step on anything
just to get that little bit higher yourself.

Jake: firewood

Finally we leave the swamp behind
and start the slow climb to Sheldon Mountain
through the forest of paperbarks.
Lucy is way out in front,
forcing the pace.
I whistle for her to slow down.
"Let's stop up ahead,
for a minute."
We sit under a tree to rest,
both leaning against the papery trunk,
looking back over the valley.
We take off our boots and socks
and dry them on a rock.
I can see the willows along Wolli Creek
and in the distance,
smoke lazily rising
from the rusted chimney at Lucy's house.
I touch her arm
and point in that direction.
Lucy says,
"Mum will be asking Peter
to go and get more firewood
and I know Peter will shout back,
'Get Lucy to do it, it's her job!'"
"Don't they know you're here?"
Lucy shrugs.
"They know nothing
and that's the way I like it."

"Will they do anything
when they find you're gone?" I ask.
"Yeah, they'll make Peter get the firewood."

Lucy: good riddance

I stretch my legs out,
feel the tension ease from my body.
Jake passes me the water bottle
and I take a long swig,
thinking of Peter having
to do some farm work,
for a change.
And Dad,
stalking around the house
looking for his beer,
saying,
"She's probably run away.
One less bloody mouth to feed.
Good riddance."
I reply, under my breath,
"Good riddance to you."

Jake: too many questions

When we start walking again
I ask Lucy,
"Does your mum or dad
ever talk about my family?"
She keeps her head down,
treading carefully along the path.
"I wouldn't know.
My parents don't say anything to me,
unless it's to tell me to do something."
I can't believe that.
"Come on. Do they?"
Lucy stops and looks at me
through her hair.
"I told you.
They don't talk to me,
and I don't talk to them."
She walks ahead
and I follow slowly.
I say, to myself,
"You must live in a quiet house."
"*What?*"
"Nothing. I was just saying …"
"I live in a dump.
That's where I live. A dump.
Are you happy now?"
I see the anger in her eyes
and hold up my hand.
"I'm sorry, Lucy.

It's just my dad ..."
I stop.
This won't help matters.
"Your dad what?"
Lucy says,
"Didn't he want you coming with me?
Because I'm a Harding.
That's probably enough reason for him."
Lucy shakes her head.
"If you want to go home,
and be with your know-all dad,
then go.
No one's stopping you."

Jake: the bush

Lucy walks deeper into the bush,
not turning around once.
I follow a few paces behind.
I'm not going back.
Not until I've proved Dad right,
or wrong.
I'm too old for wolf stories now.
It's time I found out the truth.

The land gets steeper and rockier.
Lucy and I walk slowly,
scrambling over huge boulders
on our hands and knees.
We don't talk,
aware of each sound in the forest.
Every snap of a branch
makes us stand silent and still,
straining to see what's out there.
The paperbarks give way to tall mountain ash.
The air is cold and crisp.
A cockatoo screeches, high above,
and we both jump in fright.
Lucy almost smiles, for a moment,
then she turns and follows the track.
I check my watch—midday.
We've been carrying these packs for a long time.
"Lucy. Let's stop at those rocks ahead, for lunch?"
We scurry up the rough incline.

I climb first, stretching for each hold,
until I can pull myself onto a smooth rock.
Lucy passes both packs
and I help her up.
"Egg sandwich, okay?"
"You bet. I'm starving."
She grins
and I can see she's got crooked teeth,
just like me and Mum.
It makes me like her.
My dad always joked
when he talked about Mum.
"Never trust anyone with straight teeth!"
I think my Dad's wrong about her.
Even if she is a Harding.

Jake: knives

Lucy lies back on the cool stone.
"My dad sat in front of the television last night,
sharpening his knives.
That means one of the old hens
is going to get it today.
They'll be eating a stringy boiler
for dinner, tonight.
Chicken soup tomorrow night.
The dogs get the bones."
She closes her eyes
and pulls her jacket tight around her.
I look down at her smooth skin
with the slight wrinkles around her mouth
as if she's smiling
or grimacing at the world,
I'm not sure which.
The wind is picking up.
Soon, Sheldon Mountain will be covered
in mist and cloud.
"The weather's closing in, Lucy.
Maybe we should turn back?"

"No way, Jake. I'm going on."
She lifts the pack and starts walking,
deeper into the bush.
I follow, thinking of her dad
and the sharpening knives.

Lucy: the groove

Sometimes when I walk
I get into such a groove
that my mind shuts down
and a rhythm takes over.
A sentence forms,
and no matter how much
I try to forget it,
the pace of my walking
keeps it coming back.

"My dad is an asshole."

Before I realize it,
I'm keeping time with a beat
that pushes me on,
step by step,
to the trees ahead;
a slow steady climb.

"My dad is an asshole."

I'm bouncing along
up this narrow track
not even aware of Jake
falling farther behind
with every step.

"My dad is an asshole.
My dad is an asshole."

THE MIST

Lucy: the mist

I love the mist,
the way it drips off the leaves
and coats everything with a glistening skin.
It reminds me of my favorite fantasy novel—
the *Lady of the Lake*
standing on a boat
in the middle of a veiled pond,
like a ghostly dream.
I always pictured myself on that boat,
gliding, untouchable.
With a wave of my hand
I could disappear back into the fog
from where I came.
That's the life.
Untouchable,
like a princess.
Like a wild dog.

Jake: the cold quiet

The mist closes in.
We can see ten meters
through the looming murk
and no more.
It's coldly quiet.
A fog blanket has shrouded the mountain
and dampened every sound.
No bird calls.
No insect buzz.
We're far from roads
and farms
and family
and loudmouth Peter
and the barking dogs.
Lucy and me,
creeping through this gloomy other-world.
The wallaby path gets narrower
and steeper
as we ready ourselves
for the last climb to the top.
Lucy waits for me to catch up.
She says,
"I've never been this far before."

I remember my trip here with Dad,
looking for lost sheep
and finding the ripped carcass.
Blood and fur,
matted together on the rocks.
"I have. Once."

Jake: the fall

It only takes one smooth rock,
a wet boot,
and the memory of a dead sheep.
I slip
and the weight of the pack
spins me round,
backward,
tumbling,
rolling down the hillside,
unable to stop.
There's no way to escape this crazy fall.
I keep my arms tight around my head
because all I'm thinking as I roll
is a rock and my face
coming together.
I close my eyes
as the blood rushes to my head.
Lucy is shouting out my name
so I dig my feet hard into the earth
and a bolt of pain
shoots through my ankle.
That's when I stop falling
and scream.

Jake: fractured?

I close my eyes,
grit my teeth,
and beat the ground with my fists
trying to block out the pain.
I swear,
over and over,
at myself,
at the mist,
at the bloody wolf
and my dad for believing in it,
for telling me about it.
I feel totally, absolutely helpless.

Lucy slides down the hill,
saying "shit" over and over
as if that's going to help.
When she reaches me,
she kneels down,
unties the laces
and gently removes my boot.
"Shit."
"Can you stop saying that?"
I'm shaking as I touch the lump
throbbing on the side of my ankle.
Fractured?
I have scratches on my arms and legs,
a rip in my pants,
and a cricket ball growing out of my ankle.

Lucy says, "Bloody hell!"
Despite the pain, I say,
"Thanks, Lucy. That's much better."

Lucy: shiver

I stop swearing and hold Jake's ankle
as he winces in pain.
I feel so useless,
cradling his swollen foot,
looking at his ripped clothes;
seeing him like this.
I let the weight of his foot sink into my lap
and I clutch his leg
to help him stop shaking.
We stay like this for a long time.
Neither of us knows what to do.
Finally, Jake opens his eyes
and jokes,
"Ring for an ambulance?"
I try to smile.
Jake says,
"I think you'd better go back, for help."
I shake my head.
"No, not now.
I couldn't make it home before dark
and there's no way they'd find you until tomorrow.
You can't stay here all night."
I shiver at the thought.
Jake out here in the mist,
alone on Sheldon Mountain.

Lucy: stupid

Stupid.
Why didn't I turn back when Jake wanted?
Why did I only think of myself,
wanting to go on and on forever
to get as far away as I could?
This mountain seemed a good place to come.
Any excuse to leave.

Wolf?
Who cares.
The only animal I knew
was the one I wanted to escape from.
And now?
I'll find us somewhere to shelter tonight
and tomorrow I'll take the long walk back,
straight to the Jackson farm,
and when Jake's dad sees me running ...
well, everything he thinks about the Hardings
will be right.

Jake: the crow, and the cave

A crow swoops down from the tree
and lands on the cliff edge,
not five meters away.
It looks at me
and lets out a pitiful squawk.
"I know how you feel," I say.

The crow spies something below and flaps away.
That reminds me.
We have apples, water,
Lucy's bread,
and the last of the sandwiches.
Enough for the night.
I gently touch my ankle.
It's almost swelling before my eyes.
Lucy calls a loud "coooeee" from above.
She's easing down the track,
her hair bouncing.
"Guess what I found?" she says.
"A doctor out on a bushwalk!"
"No."
"A luxury mountain resort?"
"No, silly."
"A rescue helicopter!"
Lucy laughs.
"A cave. Just up there.
It only goes a few meters into the cliff,
but it's dry,

out of the mist and the wind."
I say, "I'd prefer a helicopter.
I've always wanted a free ride."
Lucy leans down to help me up
and says,
"If you don't stop joking
I'll break your other foot."

Lucy: in the dark, in the quiet

He's holding his foot
making pathetic jokes
and I'm sure he's doing it for me.
I know how much pain he's in;
how much it hurts when things get damaged.
I put that out of my mind.
It's my fault for rushing, escaping, so quickly.
Now I have to make it right.

We'll be okay.
A night in a cave,
in the dark,
alone.
I carry Jake's pack
and help where I can
as he drags himself
up the narrow track.
When he rests,
I hold his hand
and he grips tight,
steadying himself,
breathing slow and heavy.
"It's not far now, Jake."
Wishing us into the cave.

Jake: a few hundred meters

A few hundred meters.
An hour.
Crawling,
dragging,
sweating,
and shivering
in the mist.
My fingers are numb
from digging into the dirt,
pulling myself along.
Lucy walks beside me,
leaning down to hold my hand when I rest.
"It's not far now, Jake.
Not far."
I think of the cave
and the cold
and Dad in our farmhouse
drumming his strong fingers
on the kitchen table
waiting for me,
thinking I'm lost somewhere,
with a Harding.
He'll be wrong.
I'm not lost.
And I'm glad Lucy's here.

THE CAVE

Jake: the cave

The cave is narrow
but deep enough for shelter.
I drop my bag against the wall
and slump back,
exhausted from the slow climb.
My foot throbs—
an angry pulse.
I cup my hands
and blow warmth
into my aching fingers.
Lucy stands at the entrance,
hands reaching to the roof,
looking into the misty cloud.
She's thinking the same thing as me.
Firewood.
"We won't be in darkness all night.
I've got a torch," I say.
She turns to me.
"It's too wet for firewood.
We'd smoke ourselves to death.
I'm not scared of the dark anyway."
I grin.
"That's good.
Because I'm petrified!"
Lucy says,
"Fractured ankle,
scared of the night,
no firewood.

Anything else I should know?"
"A few things,
but I'll tell you later,
when it gets really dark
and the mist creeps in,
and the wolf howls …"

We both laugh at ourselves
and our big wolf adventure.

Jake: night

Lucy sits beside me.
We're in this together.
Outside the light is fading.
We listen to the sound of water
dripping off the cave entrance.
I flash my torch
at the wall opposite,
waving it up and down.
Lucy taps my arm
and points at the beam.
"What's that?
Your cave drawing of a wolf?"
"No.
S-O-S by torchlight."
"Very good, Jake.
Pity there's no one to see it,
except me."
"You'll do.
At least you stayed, Lucy.
Your brother,
he would have left me here,
alone, waiting until morning."
"Peter would have got lost hurrying home.
You'd be a skeleton in a cave!"
"Well then,
I'm *really* glad you're here."
Lucy smiles and goes to punch my arm,
but I grab her hand and hold it tight.

She wraps her fingers in mine.
Neither of us wants to let go.
Our hands drop gently between us
and, for a moment, all I feel
as I rest against my backpack
is her warm hand in mine.

Lucy: Jake's pulse

I don't get any of this.
We're sitting next to each other
in the vanishing light
holding hands.
If anyone tried this at school
I'd slap them.
What happens now?
I'm glad it's dark in here
to hide my blushes.
Maybe this won't be so bad.
At least Jake doesn't hate me.
I lean back
and I'm surprised to feel
his pulse,
beating steady through his hand.
Or maybe it's my own heartbeat?

Imagine his dad walking in now.
Imagine my dad.
Shit.
I don't know who'd be more scared,
me or Jake.
To hell with parents.
They're not here.
Not tonight.

Lucy: in the sunshine

Sometimes when I'm alone
by Wolli Creek
in the early morning,
all I hear is a gentle ripple
of water over rocks.
I sit on the bank,
close my eyes,
and time just drifts.
Sunshine warms my body.
I swear my heart beats slower
and that's all the movement I need.
I read about meditation once.
It must be like this.
You switch off
every bad thought and memory
and all you know is warmth
settling on you.
I stay by the creek
as long as I can.
It's my place,
where no one can reach.

Sitting next to Jake,
his hand in mine,
that's like sunshine
beside Wolli Creek.

Jake: Lucy's prayer

"Jake?"
Lucy's voice is a whisper
in the ink-black stillness.
"Do you pray?
At night, for things you want?"
I can feel my heart,
beating,
tracing a blood line
down to my throbbing ankle.
I don't answer.
"Every night
I lie in bed
listening to Peter snoring
in the next room
and the dogs scuffling outside
on the creaky veranda.
I pray for impossible things.
No more wars.
No more floods
or bushfires.
Sometimes I list everything bad in the world:
kidnapping,
murder,
terrorist attacks,
car crashes,
death by lightning,
death by drowning,
and I pray for it all to stop.

I'm not sure who I'm praying to.
But alone,
on our shitty little farm,
a minute of prayer can't hurt.
Look,
it's better than what my brother does
in bed at night.
Fart-bombs.
Flapping blankets and giggling."

Lucy: my little world

I've never told anyone
what I just told Jake.
About my prayers.
I just blurted it all out.
He listened
and I think he understood.
He kept holding my hand.

As I was talking
I wondered,
am I horrible for being pleased
we're stuck here tonight?
Is that bad?
I'm sorry about his ankle
and the hurt he's got,
but I'm glad he's here.
I feel like one of those Trobriand women.
This cave is my island, my little world.
It's good.
I just want to enjoy this feeling.
This powerful feeling.

Jake: the locusts

I shine the torch
toward the cave entrance
and the impenetrable mist.
I switch it off
and we sit in the dark,
our shoulders touching.
"Do you remember the locust plague
a few years back?
After the rains,
all the paddocks were green
and the sheep were eating their fill
for the first time in months.
Remember?
Then the locusts came.
The sheep huddled under the trees,
while the grass disappeared
in a brown haze,
like wicked magic.
I was so angry
I put on my cricket helmet,
stretched mosquito net over the face guard,
took my bat,
and stood in the middle of the paddock
practicing my hook shot
until the bat was stained yellow.
It was all I could do.
Mum and Dad sat on the veranda
watching their work go bad

while I played cricket,
and lost."

"What did they say, Jake?
When you came in?"
"Dad shook my hand,
and Mum said,
'Good innings, son!'
And the next morning,
Dad was out early on his tractor,
unloading bales of hay in the paddocks,
feeding his sheep,
as if nothing had happened."

Lucy: the plague

I remember the plague too.
I was twelve.
Mum and Peter were in town.
Dad and I went out to round up
the few sheep we had left.
We spent hours in the paddock,
running back and forward,
chasing the sheep in circles,
whistling at the dogs,
locusts crashing into our faces.
Dad got madder and madder,
yelling at me;
blaming me for the wandering flock,
for the locusts,
for him being stuck on the farm.
I was running flat out
trying to get the sheep into the shed
with Martha and Winnie.

All afternoon,
running around the stupid paddock,
chasing stupid sheep,
getting splattered by stupid locusts,
with my stupid father
waving his arms like a madman,
shouting abuse—
not at his dumb sheep,
or his worthless dogs,

or the locusts—
but at *me*.
What was I to do?
Somehow I got the sheep in the shed.
I fell down on the hay,
exhausted,
while Dad kept swearing,
calling me useless.

I was twelve
for God's sake.
What did he want from me?

Jake: eucalypt

We stop talking,
exhausted by the climb
and the memories of locusts.
I drift asleep for a few moments
but the pain stirs.
I feel Lucy's hand go limp,
then squeeze,
then go limp again.
She's having a dream,
or a nightmare.
I hold her hand firm
to let her know I'm here.
I think of the wolf,
and how Dad's story has led me and Lucy
to this cave.
I don't care about my ankle.
I'm glad we came here.
Lucy's body jerks
and her legs flex
as though she wants to run.
I whisper her name
but she doesn't wake.
I lean close to her hair.
It smells of eucalypt.

Jake: on hard ground

My body feels numb
sitting on this hard ground,
helpless,
waiting out the night,
knowing the chance to find the wolf is gone.
I feel my pulse race
as the ache throbs through my body.
Now it's me who wants to howl,
in pain and frustration at being stuck here,
knowing that when I get home
Dad's going to blame Lucy
and tell me again
the Hardings are no good.
He's wrong, but how do I convince him of that?
There's more chance of him
believing the wolf is just a wild dog.
He knows what he believes.
It's up to me to prove him wrong.

Peter

She's run away, I reckon.
Don't you, Mum?
She's taken her bag
and she took food.
I was going to eat that!
Maybe she's not coming back.
Are we going to look for her?
Call the cops?
Get a search party?
Wow. That'd be really cool.
She won't be able to hide
from no search party.
We can get the dogs
to sniff her clothes.
They'll lead us right to her.
What do you think, Mum?

It's pretty late.
We don't have to go out in the dark,
do we?
Maybe we should wait till morning.
She'll come home by then.
And why is Dad just standing
in the backyard, Mum?
Staring at the hills.

Jake: stories

Lucy wakes,
pushing back her hair
and staring out at the night.
"Do you really believe
we'll see your wolf, Jake?
Honestly?"
I search long into the dark,
and think, Not tonight,
not in this cave.
But I know she's asking me
if I believe in the wolf,
believe that it exists.
"When I was growing up,
Dad loved to tell me about the wolf."
Maybe Lucy's prayers are the same
as Dad and his story.
It's what they hold onto;
it doesn't matter if they're true.

"So yes, Lucy.
My dad saw it.
That's enough for me."

In the pit of my stomach
I hope he's right,
but
he was wrong about Lucy.

Lucy: lies

When Jake says that
I get so angry,
I want to shake him and shout,
"Parents lie!
Parents say what they want
to get their own way."
I know it's no use. Jake and his dad
have their little story to fall back on.
It's not up to me to prove them wrong.
Hell.
I don't care if it's a wolf,
or a wild dog,
or a bloody ghost.
To me,
it's an excuse to leave home.
Jake can believe what he likes.
Lucky him.
I say,
"Jake, if your dad believed in Santa,
I guess you would too."
"Santa!" he says. "Not real?
How could you say such a thing?"
For a moment, I don't get it.
Then Jake shines the torch into his face
and I see him smiling, and he winks
and rolls around laughing at his joke
until he bumps his ankle and screams in pain.
"Serves yourself right!" I say.

He holds his ankle
but can't resist saying,
"It's okay.
I'll get over Santa,
eventually!"
I threaten to hit him,
but instead I lean over
and kiss him on the lips
and it's a nice kiss.
I blush
and he kisses me back
and that's a nice kiss as well.

Lucy: blushes

Bloody hell.
Where did that come from?
I've never kissed anyone before.
But, it was either hit Jake
or kiss him.
So I chose.
I hope I chose right.
It felt good too.
Kind of warm and soft
and I could feel the blood
rushing around my body,
not sure where to go,
filling up my veins with heat.
We let our lips linger
for long enough to enjoy.
I blushed
and he kissed me back.
Bloody hell.
What happens now?

THIS IS WHAT HAPPENS

Jake: what wolf?

I can smell the eucalyptus
as we kiss.
I press my face into her long hair
as we move together
without speaking.
My arms are tight
around Lucy
and we're so close
it's almost overwhelming.
The warmth,
the sweet smell of her hair,
the touch of her body inside my arms,
the sound of our breathing.

If I had a choice between
a fractured ankle and
a night in the cave with Lucy
or
a guarantee to find the wolf,
I'd look at myself in the mirror
and say,
"Wolf? What wolf?"

Lucy: for good

This is what happens.
One thing,
one simple thing.
And you know
when it happens
that it's going to break
everything that's come before.
I know it.
I can tell.

Don't laugh at me,
like I'm a dumb teenager
with my first kiss.
That's bullshit.

I've seen things
that I knew, there and then,
were going to get to me.
I've seen bad
thundering through our house
and it made my stomach churn
and every muscle in my body
grow tense like cold wire.
I've hidden under the house
in the dirt
like a cornered animal
waiting for the jaws
to snap shut.

I was powerless to stop his rampage.

I don't want to feel like that anymore.

That kiss from Jakc changes everything.
It changes everything for good.

Jake: it doesn't matter

Lucy stands
and walks into the darkness
at the back of the cave.
It's so quiet I can hear her breathing.
She says,
"I lied, Jake.
About knowing where the wolf lived.
I'm sorry.
I thought if there was a wolf,
he'd live somewhere like here.
I didn't come looking for your wolf."

I've spent years dreaming about his lair.
I knew he prowled Beaumont Hill
searching for food,
or a mate,
but when Lucy told me of Sheldon Mountain,
it seemed right.
Somewhere mysterious,
hidden from everyone.
I wanted to find the wolf.
To prove it to myself,
and to Dad.
But now, maybe it doesn't matter.
I'm glad Lucy's here,
even if she didn't come for the wolf.
"Lucy, why?"

Lucy: the soaking

I gently place my backpack under Jake's heel
to give him something to rest his ankle on.
I lean in close to tell him a story,
to explain ...

"One day, last year,
I was walking home from Hopkins Bridge.
Thunder rumbled over Beaumont Hill
as the rain poured down.
I was in for a soaking,
with nowhere to hide.
Suddenly,
lightning struck a tree
in the paddock right beside me.
It split the tree in two
as if it was kindling
falling across the track
with a sad creaking dive.
I could have run;
Peter would have,
crying all the way home.

"You know what I did?
I walked to the paddock
where the tree was struck.
I lay down in the bristling wet grass
and watched the clouds battle across the sky.
Have you ever watched raindrops

falling straight toward you?
It's like you're lifted into the storm.
There's just you and the sky.
I wasn't scared.
I was *in* the storm.
It was freedom.
It was worth the soaking.

"I wanted to be free, Jake."

Jake: real

I'm a normal teenage boy.
I look at all the girls
on television,
in movies,
in soaps,
in magazines.
These girls with their clean hair,
gleaming white teeth
and flawless skin,
they shine like glossy varnish
has been painted on them.
Lucy didn't feel like I imagined.
She felt soft
and firm
at the same time
and as we kissed
I felt her getting warmer,
responding to me.
It was the most magical thing
I've ever known.
Lucy is beautiful,
but not like those fantasy girls.
Lucy is real.

Jake: Lucy and me

When Lucy held her hair back
I leaned in close
and started kissing her again.
Simple.
I'm not saying much more
about what we did.
You don't tell people those things.
It's not right, to say.
We lay there,
kissing,
getting warmer,
and everything in my past
just disappeared:
the farm and the long driveway,
the hen house and the eggs every morning,
Mum drinking tea on the veranda,
Patch and Spud barking,
the magpies ringing from the trees,
Wolli Creek bubbling over the rocks,
Dad coming in from the paddocks, humming,
the wolf,
all gone.
It was Lucy and me.
It was like getting lost in the bush
and being happy to wander;
to enjoy the sounds and smells
and to touch each tree, each shrub.
I don't care if it doesn't make sense.
It's how I feel.
It's Lucy and me.

Lucy: think good things

I'm not telling anybody anything.
Think what you like,
why would I care?
Jake and me
did what we did.

If only you could see
the grin on my face.
I'm glad it's dark
so I can smile away to myself
like some half-crazy fool.

And I know why Jake's dad
looks after his farm and his family.
It came to me
when Jake and me were …
you know.
It's the place where good things happen,
where you feel at home.
Sacred ground, if you like.
And, for me, that's this cave.

I'm not saying everything is rosy now.
Nothing's that easy.
But, now I know,
I'm normal.
Maybe a little special.

At least, special to someone.

I'm not saying anything more.
You can imagine it.

Lucy: one smart old lady

Grandma once told me
Mum didn't want to marry Dad,
she had to.
Pregnant.
With me.
He was some wild boy passing through.
And because Grandpa didn't approve,
they had to live in town until I was born.
Then Grandma took pity on us
after Grandpa died
and made us come and live on the farm.
Me a little baby
and Mum learning to be a mum.
And Dad?
He spent all day in the yard,
smoking and sitting around
waiting for nothing to happen.
Grandma ran the farm
like she always had,
even when Grandpa was alive.

And like the locust plague,
we settled on the farm
and made it our own.
Me and Superman grew up,
wondering why Dad and Grandma
didn't talk much to each other.
But then Grandma,
she was always one smart old lady.

Lucy: what do I say?

I kneel down beside Jake
and say what I've got to say,
about parents.
I start with slaps
turning into the leather strap
hard across my legs.
I don't stop.
I say more than I meant to
and less than I want,
but enough.
Jake doesn't move,
his arm around my shoulder,
as I speak in this urgent whisper
until it's all done.
And then I cry.
You won't believe this:
I've never cried in front of someone.
Never.
I used to think it was weakness.
And now I've started, I don't stop.
Jake holds me gently.
I cry years' worth of tears
in one night.
Jake keeps holding me,
whispering,
"Lucy,"
over and over.
I feel better
hearing Jake's voice
and my name.

Jake: real pain

What Lucy is feeling,
that's real pain.
The sort that stabs and pounds
and makes you shake with anger.
My ankle, it's just an injury.
It'll go away in a few weeks
and I'll probably never think of it again.
I stroke Lucy's hair
and repeat her name,
hoping my voice can ease the hurt.
I hold her in my arms
where she's safe
and I try hard not to think about tomorrow
when she'll have to go home
because of me
and my useless ankle.

Lucy: dreams

It seems like ages,
but finally I fall asleep
and dream of being far away.
I'm on my island
with Jake
and we're swimming in a clear lagoon
and yes, there are coconuts and palm trees
and we're naked!
Can you believe that?
Swimming in warm water
without a stitch on.
The sand is blinding white
under our toes
and we can see rainbow fish.
You can say all you like
about me reading too many books
and dreaming of the Trobriands—
the islands, I mean,
not the sex-mad girls!
I don't care.
It was a good dream.
It was a dream you should have
when you're sixteen years old.
It was a dream with Jake in it.
Jake and me.
It was better than most dreams I've had.

Jake: close by

Lucy's head snuggles
into my shoulder.
I can just see the outline of her face
and her hair falling across my jacket.
I don't mind how long she sleeps.
I'm happy to be close by her,
for as long as she wants.
I've never slept beside anyone before.

Tonight is a first for lots of things.
I want to hold that feeling
as long as possible.
Lucy rolls gently onto her side
and puts her arm around me.
I close my eyes,
and all I see is her face,
all I hear is her breath,
all I feel is her touch.
I go back to sleep,
happy to be here.

9

MORNING

Lucy: nightmare

A shout!
I wake in panic.
Did I hear a cry from the forest?
I crawl to the entrance
and listen—
a faint breeze shivers the leaves.
The mist is clearing.
Somebody, something is out there,
maybe staring back at me,
watching, waiting.
Jake's steady breathing
comes from the dark.
Do I answer?
If I call out I'll scare Jake.

Was it a nightmare?
What if it's him, hunting for me?
Dad blundering about in the bush,
getting angrier with every stumble.
I peer into the murky darkness,
wanting to shout,
"You can't find me.
You can't touch me.
You can't hurt me anymore."
He's a menace,
a shadow slouching behind me today
when I hurry back to Jake's farm
to get help.

But I won't let him find me.
I hope he gets lost in the dense woods
and never makes his way out.
Let him feel small.
Let him know what it's like to be scared.

Lucy: the muffled sound

A muffled sound rises from the valley
and a rush of wind shakes the trees.
A branch snaps.
Someone *is* out there,
moving below me.
I stare into the gloom
and see a flash in the distance.
Torchlight!
He's out there, searching for me.
What if he finds this cave?
Jake and me?

I crawl back inside,
my nightmare becoming real.
Getting closer.
No!
I shut my eyes tight
against the forest
and its invader.
I wrap my arms around Jake,
gently over his sleeping body.

He won't find me with Jake.
I shudder at the thought of what he'd do.
He can't see us together.

I whisper,
"I'm leaving to get help.

You sleep. I'll be back with your dad."
Jake grunts, half asleep.

I won't let him find me here.
I'll face him alone,
if I have to.

Lucy: the shadows

I leave Jake with the food and water,
move slowly to the entrance
and step out into the first hint of morning.
I inch down the track, carefully,
remembering Jake's fall,
yesterday.
So long ago.
At the bottom of the hill,
I take a deep breath
and plunge into the forest,
ready for anything.

I pick up a fallen branch
as thick as my arm.
I need something to hold,
to give me courage.
A walking stick, I tell myself.
I follow the track,
slowly picking my way through the undergrowth.
Every step I take is closer to him,
standing there, flashing his torch,
and grinning.
Smug because he's got me.

I grip the branch and stop.
He won't find me.
I'm smarter than he is.
There's a way to outwit him.

I know he'll keep to the track.
I'm sure of it.
He'll be too scared of getting lost in the bush
and lumbering about for ages.

It's simple.
I won't take the track.
I'll do what every animal does.
There's safety in the bush.
If I keep the first glow of the sun in front of me,
slightly to my right,
I'll be heading toward home.
I push into the forest
that gives me cover
and a chance to escape.

Lucy listens

The hardest part
is listening to every sound,
waiting for him to appear from behind a tree
near the track,
wet and furious,
and both of us
miles from anywhere.
My step quickens.
I try to get into a rhythm—
"My dad is an asshole,
my dad is an asshole"—
but it doesn't work.
All it does is bring him closer
in these lonely woods.
He lurks,
a scowl tattooed across his face,
and all I can do
to stop him becoming real
is keep my eyes down
and pick my way through
the overbearing bush.
He waits for me
around every corner.

Lucy: a presence

Suddenly,
I feel a presence.
My body tenses.
I'm being watched.
I search in the half-light
for a movement through the trees.

A silence creeps through the forest
and I grip the branch tighter.
I crouch, better to stay hidden,
and try to slow my breathing.
If he comes closer
I'll have to decide whether to run
or face him,
here,
alone in the bush.

For a second I close my eyes
and see Jake, still asleep,
curled in the cave,
his head on my backpack.
He's dreaming of the wolf
standing at the cave entrance.
I hope his dream comes true.

I can't stay here much longer,
hiding.
Something is out there.

I have to stand and face it
or else I'll never move.
I push the branch into the ground
and raise myself to the forest
and its presence.

Lucy: like a stray wolf

There!
Near the trees.
A movement.

Please don't let him see me.
I can't escape, or attack.

It's an animal.
A dog, or a …
Moving slowly near the track,
he stops and smells my scent.
He looks straight at me.

A silhouette in the tall grass.
He's not scared and neither am I.

We take a step toward each other,
inquisitive,
as if pulled by some timeless bond.
In that moment,
my fear falls away
and I'm lost in his eyes.
How long has he been out here,
searching?
We stand facing each other.
The wild dog and me.
Slowly, carefully, I kneel down
to be at his level.

"Are you Shadow?
Or the wolf?"
The dog moves forward
in response to my voice,
his tongue out,
head down,
eyes never leaving me.
His fur is grizzled gray and black.
I reach my hand out,
beckoning.
"Come closer.
Let me get a better look."
The dog bounds sideways
into the bush and is gone.

I fall to my knees
and for a few minutes
I can't possibly move.
I've seen him.
He's out here,
like Jake said he was.
I don't know what to do.
Go back to Jake and the cave
and tell him what I saw?
Or keep going, for help?

I can still picture him
standing there, looking at me,

without making a sound.
Like a ghost.
That's why Jake's dad tells his story,
over and over.
He saw the wolf
and telling his story keeps it real.
Gives him strength.

I stand straight,
every muscle tingling,
sure I can go on, ready for what I must do.
I follow the track away from the cave,
deeper into the woods.
Like the stray wolf,
I'm not alone

Lucy: Grandma

"Time only goes one way."
That's what Grandma
used to say.
Every time I'd sit with her
on the veranda
and tell her about school,
Peter and his annoying ways,
Mum not standing up for herself,
or Dad and his temper,
she'd just sit there and
point her walking stick
at the farmyard gate,
as if wishing it open.
I knew she wasn't talking
about waiting to die.
She was telling me
to hold tight,
to wait,
that it'll all pass.
I'd follow her eyes
to the gate
and I'd whisper,
"Time only goes one way."

When she died,
I wanted to put it
on her headstone,
up on the hill.

But no one listened to me,
except Grandma,
and she was gone.

Lucy: fractured sounds bad

The sky is early-morning blue
and you could get lost in it.
I see the vapor trail of a jet miles above
and for once
I don't wish I was escaping on it.
I'm returning along the track
to Jake's farm
to get help.
What will I say?
How much will I say?
Jake's voice echoes,
"Just tell them I'm all right,
I've hurt my ankle.
Don't say anything is fractured.
That sounds bad."

I wonder what he's doing now?
I laugh out loud as I picture Jake
sitting at the cave entrance,
his eyes searching the valley below,
looking for the wolf.
I'll tell him as soon as I get back.
The calm I felt when I saw the wolf;
the power he gave me.

Lucy: the plan

As I enter the swamp
I see a boot print
and I know it's his—
the weight,
the markings.
He's looking for me,
carrying a torch
and all that hatred.
The print is heading home
and I can imagine him now
sitting under the tree,
ignoring Peter and Mum,
knowing I've got to come back
sooner or later;
waiting for his chance.

I don't care what happens
when I get home.
I mean it.
Dad can hit me again.
He can try.
Only this time I won't run.
I won't put my hands up.
I'll stand straight,
just out of his reach.
Even though my legs
will be shaking
and my insides churning,

I won't move.
I'll keep my eyes fixed on Mum
and see what she does.
I don't care anymore.

What Jake and I got.
That can't be touched;
it can't be broken.
My father can bash me
all he likes,
but I know now,
he can't touch me.
I'm unbreakable.
I'm strong.
Stronger than any fist.

Lucy: not alone

Maybe that's my dad's problem.
That's why he's always angry;
why he hits before he thinks.
Because he doesn't believe.
Because he's got nothing to hold onto,
deep down,
nothing that makes him a man.
What must it be like
to be so alone,
so unloved.
No,
I'm not feeling sorry for him.
I'm not that forgiving.

But I know that
I've got Jake
and the cave
and the wild dog—
the wolf—
whatever it is.
And my dad,
he's got nothing.

Lucy: Jake's dad

Jake's dad!
He's walking along the track
beside the creek,
leading a horse;
his head down,
looking for tracks.
He kneels
and touches the ground
like he's trying to feel for his son.
I'm about to call his name
when he looks up.
His hand goes straight to his heart
as if to stop it leaping out of his chest.
I start running.
I don't want to look worried,
or in a panic,
but I run so I reach him quickly
and when I get there
I see the suspicion on his face.
I've done something bad to his son;
I'm a Harding.

"He's okay, Mr. Jackson," I say.
"Just a sprained ankle.
We stayed in a cave last night.
I came to get help."

He listens to the story
of Jake slipping on the rock
and how instead of walking home on the ankle
and making it worse,
we decided to find shelter
and get help in the morning.
He nods and asks,
"How are you, Lucy?"
No one has ever asked about me.
I don't know how to answer
or how to trust anyone's questions.
I say,
"Let's go get Jake."

Lucy: how happy

Jake's dad doesn't say much
as we head to Sheldon Mountain.
He asks me
if I'd like to ride the horse,
to rest,
but I say,
"No, I don't want to be a burden."
He looks at me.
"Burden?"
Then he seems to lose track
of what he wanted to say.
I'm relieved.
I just want to find Jake
and get this over with.

The sun is high
when we reach the bottom of the mountain.
Mr. Jackson ties the horse's reins
to an old gum tree
and loads his pack
with food and water
for the climb.
As we set off over the rocks
I think of Jake,
sitting, waiting,
and how happy he'll be
when he sees his dad.

How happy he'll be.

Peter

Mum, you gotta come,
quick.
Dad's gone.
And so is the car.
Has he gone looking for Lucy?
But why would he take the car?
He won't get far over the paddocks in that.
Why didn't he take the bike?
Why didn't he wait for me?
The dogs, Mum,
they're still chained up.
They'll find Lucy.
It don't make sense, Mum.
And I checked too,
Dad's gun is still there.
He don't go anywhere without his gun.
I reckon it would be handy.
He could fire off a shot
and Lucy would hear it miles away,
don't you reckon?
So why no gun?
And the car?
Where's he gone, Mum?
I want to find Lucy.
I want to find Dad.

Lucy: hungry

We reach Jake
soon after midday.
Yes, he's sitting on the rock,
his foot resting on the pack.
When he sees his dad
he scrambles to his feet
and stumbles into his father's arms.
I hang back near the cave
and watch them
with their eyes closed,
hugging.
They stay like that for a long time
and it's like they're fixing something
that almost got broke.
You know what I mean?
They're saying stuff without a word
and so I keep real quiet.
When they stop,
Jake limps over
and puts his arms around me.
He says "thanks,"
even though he doesn't need to.
He kisses me
right there in front of his dad
and all Mr. Jackson says is,
"You must both be hungry.
Let's eat."

Lucy: ghosts

I finish my sandwich
and drink some water.
Jake and his dad are close together,
on the rock.
I can't wait any longer.

"I saw the wolf."

His father slowly grins
and I'm sure he wants to say,
"I knew it. I knew it."

"It was in the forest this morning.
He was right in front of me
and everything was quiet and still,
like a dream.
Can you believe it?
Just me and him!
I don't know if it was a wolf
or a wild dog.
He was in the long grass,
but he was big.
When he moved away,
he was silent,
like a ghost."
My voice trails off
as I look into the forest below
where the wolf lives,

and prowls.
I saw what I saw;
they can believe me
or not.
Jake's dad rubs his forehead,
lost in thought.
Jake says,
"He's our wolf, Dad."

Lucy: Jake's dad

Jake's dad starts packing,
giving himself time to gather his thoughts.
"I believe in the wolf, Lucy.
I have since that day
beside Wolli Creek."

He scratches a stick into the ground.
"But when Jake didn't come home last night,
I knew deep in my bones
he was out here,
somewhere in the forest,
looking for the wolf."
He draws a cross
with the stick
over and over
unaware he's doing it.
"I felt sick, Jake.
I'd put you at risk,
because of my obsession."
He stands and tosses the stick
over the ledge.
"Who cares if it's a wolf,
a feral dog,
a dingo-cross,
a huge fox,
or, yes, even a ghost!
Who cares?
The bloody thing eats my sheep

and howls at night.
That's enough to know.
I'm sorry, Jake.
So sorry.
I didn't mean for you
to go looking for my wolf."

Jake: what matters

Maybe I came here to prove Dad wrong.
If all we found was a wild dog,
I could tell Dad he was mistaken.
If there really was a wolf,
well,
it would become *my* wolf.
Because I saw him,
I found him.

"No, Dad. I had to come.
I wanted to find what was out here."
I hold out my hand
for Lucy to help me up.
I'm just like Dad.
I want to be right,
all the time.
Lucy looks from me to Dad
and says,
"What you believe in, Mr. Jackson,
that's all there is."

Dad nods, smiles
and reaches for my hand,
to help me down the track.

It's time to leave
Sheldon Mountain.

Jake: Wolli Creek

On the slow walk to Wolli Creek,
Dad and Lucy swap stories,
going into every detail of their sightings,
and I realize that, from now on,
there is no escaping the wolf.

We sit beside the stream
in the late afternoon sunshine.
My ankle throbs
with the pain
of the scramble down
Sheldon Mountain
to Charlie.
We're nearly home.
Lucy is holding a shiny rock
in her hands, turning it over and over,
and looking out across the creek
to her farmhouse.
"You can come home with us, Lucy,"
I say.
"If you want, I'll go with you tomorrow,
to your place."

Lucy tosses the rock
into the water,
watching the ripples
slowly spread.
"Thanks, Jake.

I'll be all right.
If I stay away too long,
Peter will have no one to annoy."

Dad looks at me,
but knows not to ask.
I reach out for Lucy's hand.
"I'll visit soon as I can,
on Charlie! Okay?"

Lucy: on the hill

I circle the yard
like a lonesome wolf
and climb up the hill to the graves.
I sit beside Grandma
and pull the weeds,
clearing around her headstone.
"Time only goes one way, Grandma.
Now I have to face him,
face them both."
I wish she was still here,
waving her cane,
sticking up for me.
I look down on our ramshackle house.
So quiet.
The dogs are asleep
under the veranda
and there are no lights on
even though it's almost dark.
Are they out looking for me?
I scoff loudly.
My voice wakes the dogs
and they start barking.
Bloody hell.
I say,
"See you, Grandma"
as I walk down the path.

Lucy: sorry

It has to be Peter
who sees me first.
Superman shouts my name,
and yells to Mum,
"I found her.
I found her!"
Yeah, good job, Superman,
you searched the backyard
and found your sister,
walking home
from Grandma's grave,
looking down at the old farmhouse.
Peter runs to me
and wraps his arms tight around me,
for God's sake.
Peter hugs me!
So I squeeze him back
and watch as Mum walks across the yard,
the tea towel still in her hands.
She hesitates as we meet
and I say,
"Sorry, Mum.
I didn't mean to worry you."
She reaches for me
and starts to cry
and keeps saying
"Sorry"
over and over,
in a frantic whisper.
"Sorry."

Lucy: no more

We stand together
with Mum squeezing my hand
as if afraid to let go
while I tell my story
of Jake and the cave,
the fall and his fractured ankle.
I don't mention the wolf.
Mum turns to lead me toward the house,
but I hold firm.
"No, Mum. No more."
I can't go inside.
Not with him there.
Mum lowers her eyes.
"He's gone, Lucy.
Gone, for good."
At that moment
all the breath rushes from me,
like falling out of a tree
and landing flat on my back.
I almost faint
with the pressure.

10

HOME

Lucy: home

Mum calls me into the kitchen,
away from Peter's questions,
and asks me to help her cook dinner.
I sit at the table and cut the vegetables
into long, thin strips.
She peels the potatoes in the sink,
keeping her voice low as she talks.
"Last night
he went looking for you, Lucy.
He was gone all night.
I sat here praying he wouldn't find you."
Mum looks up, quickly.
"Not because I didn't want you home.
It wasn't that.
I didn't want him to hurt you again.
He came back at dawn,
swearing and shouting."
Mum grips the peeler tightly,
scraping away the skin of each potato
with sharp angry strokes.
"You were right, Lucy.
You can't just keep out of his way."
She leans on the bench
and I'm worried she's going to faint.
"When he returned,
I grabbed his arm.
Can you believe it, Lucy?
I led him outside,

away from Peter, sleeping.
I stood in the yard,
the keys to the car in my hand."
Mum puts down the peeler
and looks at me.
"I'm sorry, Lucy.
I'm not proud of this,
but I said,
'One of us has to leave.'
I didn't want it to be me.
I dropped the car keys between us
and waited.
He sneered—
you know, like he always does—
and said,
'If I pick them up, that's it.
I'm never coming back.'
I turned and walked inside.
I was shaking, Lucy.
It was like time was standing still
until I heard the motor start.
Then I cried and cried.
Here in the kitchen.
It was all I could do
to not howl, Lucy.
I sat here listening for you.
I was so afraid I'd lost you forever,
even though I knew you'd be safe.

You have a touch of Grandma in you."

Mum looks toward the lounge room.
I know she's thinking,
What does Peter have?
I put my arms around her.
"Peter has us, Mum."

Peter

My sister went looking for their wolf.
Jake and her
got stuck in a cave
and stayed the night
in the dark.
How cool would that have been?
But they never found nothing.
Dad went looking for her
and he found nothing, too.
I don't know why he left.
It's not fair.
He didn't tell me.
He just snuck off
when I was asleep.
I kept asking Mum all morning
but she didn't say much that made sense to me.
Maybe he just got sick of sitting round the farm
where it's boring and nothing happens.
Maybe he's gone to be a truckie again.
But he still should have said goodbye.
He should have said something.

Lucy: dinner

We cook a roast—
the first we've had since Winnie died—
with baked potatoes
and dumplings and gravy,
and Peter keeps asking for more.
Superman needs to build up his strength
now he's the man of the house,
which makes me smile
and almost laugh out loud.
But I can't do that
because Peter misses him,
and he doesn't understand why Dad's gone.
We're going to have to tell him.
It won't be easy.

As Mum carves the meat
right down to the bone,
and pours the thick gravy,
we glance at each other.
I want to ask her something,
but it's too soon.
Mum says,
"I hope you like the dinner."
She glances toward Dad's chair
as if she's said too much.
"It's fine, Mum."
She forces a smile
and offers me more.

Lucy: Grandma's candle

My grandma
used to burn a long white candle
beside her bed
early on Sunday morning.
She'd close her eyes
and whisper to Grandpa,
who'd been gone for years.
In the silence I knew he was answering,
sending back his love.
She said the smell of the candle
brought them together
and as long as that candle flamed
no one could intrude.

After dinner
I go into Grandma's room
and find a scented candle in the drawer
beside her bed.
I take it to the window,
light it,
and place it on the ledge
where I can see their graves.

I tell her about the cave—
Jake and me,
what we did,
what we said.
And I tell her about the wild dog,

the wolf,
roaming the hills,
and I pray he finds a partner.
I breathe in the vanilla smoke
and close my eyes.
I can see her face.
Grandma once said,
"Some people are born half-dead.
And they take years to go."

"Not me, Grandma.
I won't ever be like that."
A full moon is rising over the tree line.
I reckon Jake is sitting at his window now,
watching the moon,
listening for a howl.

Lucy: this house

I open the door to Grandma's room
and let the candle scent drift through the house.
I follow its cleansing perfume,
the floorboards creaking with every step.
Peter snores
and the dogs scuffle around outside.
In the lounge room is my father's chair,
big and comfortable.
I sit in it and lean back,
put my feet on the coffee table,
stare at the wide plank walls
and the high patterned ceiling
that I'd never noticed before.
Grandma's house.
I fall asleep
in my father's chair
and I don't dream.

I sleep long into the morning
until a movement wakes me.
Peter is standing beside me,
his hair all messy from bed.
He says,
"That's Dad's chair."

I want to say,
"Not anymore"
but I stop myself.

This house,
this room,
these walls,
they've heard enough arguing.

Jake: Lucy smiles

Mum and Dad
are mending the fence
in the eastern paddock.
If I was there, I'd be tightening the wire, slowly,
while Dad's big hands check the tension.
But I'm sitting on the veranda,
ankle bandaged, leg raised,
watching the cockatoos
in the old dead tree.
I don't notice Lucy
coming across the yard.
She says, "Hi, Jake,"
and I almost fall off my chair.
She giggles and says,
"Sorry, I didn't mean to scare you."
She stands at the foot of the stairs,
her hands deep in her pockets.
I tell her I've been scanning Wolli Creek
waiting for the wolf.
I hold up my binoculars
to prove I'm serious
even though,
truth be known,
I'm just doing it
because there's not much else to do
with one foot tightly bandaged
and orders from Mum
to keep off it.

Lucy sits beside me on the lounge
and feels the soft cushions.
"It's more comfortable than the cave,
but not as much fun."
I'm not sure who blushes more.
She leans in close
and we kiss,
just quickly.
Her hair is tied back in a long ponytail
with a dark blue ribbon.
"I like your hair, Lucy."
She smiles.
Lucy smiles
on our veranda.

Lucy: I will

I sit beside Jake
as we watch the sun
fade slowly behind
Beaumont Hill.
The deepest, brightest orange
shines through the high clouds
and it's beautiful.
It's perfect.
I tell Jake about Mum,
how she stood up to him at last
and kept saying Sorry all night
until the word was worn out.
I didn't want to talk about the past anymore.
We agreed not to mention him again.
Mum said,
"Let's just get on with it, Lucy."
And the voice wasn't Mum,
it was Grandma.
It was her way of dealing with droughts,
or floods,
or fire.
She'd stand on the veranda,
arms folded, her eyes sparkling,
and she'd say,
"Let's get on with it."
And we would.
So, I will.